THE
CHANGELING

Malachy Doyle
Jac Jones

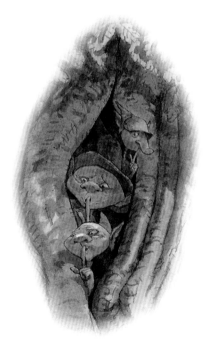

For Liam

First Impression—1999
Second Impression—2002

ISBN 1 85902 691 5

© text: Malachy Doyle
© illustrations: Jac Jones

Malachy Doyle and Jac Jones have asserted their rights under the Copyright, Designs and Patents Act, 1988, to be identified as
Author and Illustrator of this Work.

This book is published with the support of the Arts Council of Wales.

Printed in Wales at
Gomer Press, Llandysul, Ceredigion

There's a big oak tree halfway up the hill between Llangurig and Llanidloes and nearby stands a farmhouse with the strangest name. It's called Y Tylwyth Teg, or The Fairy Folk.

Some years ago Twm and Gwyneth lived there and they longed for a child, so they were thrilled when Gwyneth gave birth to two fine healthy boys, dark-haired Huw and fair-haired Ifan.

One evening when Twm was out in the fields, Gwyneth found that all the milk in the house had turned sour.

'That's odd,' she said to herself. 'I'd better run down and borrow some from Old Nerys, or Huw and Ifan will cry all night.'

She put on her coat and kissed her sleeping babies. 'I'll only be gone a few minutes,' she whispered.

'Could you spare any milk for the twins, Nerys?' she asked, arriving at the cottage.

'I could of course, Gwyneth,' said the old woman, filling a jug. 'But you shouldn't be leaving your children alone with darkness falling. Surely you've heard of the Tylwyth Teg and their fondness for little fair-haired boys?'

'Oh, don't be silly, Nerys,' said Gwyneth, lightly. 'No one believes in those old tales any more.'

Nearing home, Gwyneth thought she saw strange shadows lurking in the blackthorn hedge. She hurried to the farmhouse but there were the twins, sound asleep in their cot.

As she warmed the milk she laughed at herself for letting the old woman frighten her.

Gwyneth heard the horse thrashing about in the stable and ran from the kitchen to see what was wrong. A few quiet words and soothing strokes and the old mare was calm again.

Next there was a great moaning and groaning from the cowhouse. Hurrying across the yard, Gwyneth opened the half door and spoke gently to the cattle until they were quiet.

As she entered the house again Siani the terrier barked wildly, and Megan the marmalade cat arched her back and hissed.

'Settle down, you two,' said Gwyneth, laughing. 'What's the matter with all my animals tonight? I suppose Old Nerys would say you're bewitched!'

'M-ma-mam,' a thin little voice whined from the corner.

Gwyneth ran to pick up Ifan. 'What a clever boy,' she crooned, for it was the first word either child had spoken. As she cradled him in her arms, Twm came in.

'D-da-dad,' said the squeaky voice, and Twm looked closely at Ifan.

'There's something the matter with that boy,' he said to his wife.

'What do you mean?' asked Gwyneth.

'Well surely he's much too young to be talking,' Twm replied.

'Nonsense,' said Gwyneth, crossly. 'It just goes to show how bright he is.'

Huw grew strong and happy but Ifan stopped growing altogether. He cried half the day and three quarters of the night, and neither milk nor lullabies would settle him.

'How am I supposed to work all day when that child keeps me awake all night?' asked Twm one morning. 'Why's he not more like his brother?'

'Don't blame Ifan,' said Gwyneth, trying to feed the little fellow one more time. 'It's not his fault he can't sleep.'

'I told you before, Gwyneth,' snapped Twm, 'I'm sure there's something wrong with him.'

'And I'm sure there's not!' shouted Gwyneth, afraid to admit it even to herself.

Twm stamped his foot and strode off to the fields without even kissing his wife goodbye, and Gwyneth burst into tears.

She stared at the children and wondered. Ifan was different, there was no doubt about it. His eyes had gone from blue to green and his hair was turning, strangely turning. Such changes often happened to babies, Gwyneth knew, but why was his face so long and thin and why were his eyes so sad?

'Maybe you're right, Twm,' said Gwyneth later, when they'd both calmed down. 'Maybe there is something wrong. Do you think I should take him to the doctor?'

'Why don't we ask Old Nerys first?' Twm suggested. 'She knows everything about everything.'

The old woman listened to their story and took a long, hard look at Ifan.

'I very much hope I'm mistaken,' she said, slowly, 'but I'd say he has the look of a changeling about him.'

'What do you mean?' asked Gwyneth, a cold shiver running down her spine.

'I mean,' said Nerys, sadly, 'that the Tylwyth Teg may have stolen away your child and left one of theirs.'

Twm gasped, and the colour drained from Gwyneth's face.

'It's the prettiest ones they take, before they've been christened,' continued the old woman, gently. 'Did you make a cross of iron and hang it round the boy's neck, Twm?'

'I didn't,' said Twm, comforting his trembling wife.

'That's a pity,' said Nerys, shaking her head. 'For it's said to keep them away.'

'So how can we be sure if he's a changeling?' asked Gwyneth desperately. 'I have to know!'

'First you must do as I tell you,' said Nerys, kindly. 'And then you must listen closely whenever he speaks. If he knows things a child could never know, you have the proof.'

It was with heavy hearts that they trudged up the lane, back to their cottage. Twm and Gwyneth were silent, and only little Huw, who knew no better, was happy. He held out his arms to be carried, and his father, sighing, lifted him up onto his shoulders, where Huw giggled merrily as he bounced along.

'Oh, Twm,' said Gwyneth, sadly, 'I'm so worried.'

'I know, love,' said Twm, 'so am I, for I cannot bear it to think of our darling boy, lost to the fairies.' He turned to look at the child in his wife's arms, who had begun to cry once more. 'And if that poor little scrap you've got there really is one of the Tylwyth Teg, as Nerys says, then the sooner they take him back the better, for I don't see him ever being happy here.'

It was the time of year for the men to be cutting hay and it was Gwyneth's job to feed them. So the next day when the sun was high in the sky, she cracked a dozen eggs, just as Nerys had told her, and put the shells on a tray on the kitchen table while she made some stew.

'Wh-wh-what are you doing, Mam?' whined the little fellow, watching her every move.

'Wait and see, child,' said Gwyneth. 'Wait and see.'

When the stew was ready she poured it into the eggshells and carried the tray to the door.

'Twm,' she called, 'bring the men in for their dinner!'

No sooner had she done so than the thin little voice piped up from the corner,

'Acorn before an oak I knew,
 And an egg before a hen,
 But I never heard of an eggshell stew
 As a dinner for harvest men!'

'Aha!' cried Gwyneth, for this was the proof she'd been waiting for. 'If you knew the acorn that our great oak tree grew from, then you must be two hundred years old if you're a day, Changeling!'

She was on the point of leaping into the clearing to fetch him but Old Nerys held her back.

'No, Gwyneth!' she whispered, fiercely. 'Don't enter that ring or you'll never get out again.'

But Gwyneth would not be stopped. 'Tylwyth Teg!' she cried, tearing herself from the old woman's grip and stepping forward. 'Give me back my own child, for he can never be happy with you!'

The dancing stopped and every fairy stared at her. Never before had a human dared to challenge them.

'Bring him here!' Gwyneth called, afraid no longer. 'And take your poor little changeling away, for it is cruel to leave him in the land of humans.'

Slowly, as though every step was painful to her, one fairy came closer. She was a beautiful fairy queen, and tightly in her arms she held Ifan. Gwyneth gasped, for now that he was nearer she could see that he looked just like Huw, only sadder, thinner and more fair.

'He is lovely,' the fairy whispered, holding him close. 'I cannot bear to let him go.'

'Yes, he is lovely,' said Gwyneth, firmly. 'But he is mine, and you must give him back!'

'Yours are so much more beautiful,' sighed the fairy. She looked past Gwyneth at the sleeping Huw. 'If I cannot have this one, could I have that one instead?'

'No!' answered Gwyneth firmly, holding out the changeling. 'This is your child! He needs your love, as Huw and Ifan need mine. The more you love him, the more beautiful he will become to you. Take him back and give me my own.'

Meanwhile the changeling had spotted his mother. As his sad crying stopped and a thin little smile spread across his face, the fairy queen's heart began to melt.

Reluctantly, she let Ifan go and took the changeling in her arms.

Ifan ran to his mother, leaping into her outstretched arms, and the young woman knew beyond the slightest doubt that it was her own son, safe and well. Twm and Huw danced with delight, before smothering Ifan in kisses, laughing and weeping in turn.

And when at last they looked up the Tylwyth Teg had gone, into the shadows and away, taking their changeling with them. The only sign they left behind was a fairy ring, made from the marks of their dancing feet.

Back at the farmhouse, Gwyneth put the children to bed, where, tired and happy, they were soon fast asleep.

And although it was the middle of the night, Twm went out to his workshop, made a pair of iron crosses and hung one around each boy's neck.

Twm and Gwyneth named the cottage Y Tylwyth Teg to remind them to keep on the right side of the fairies, and Huw and Ifan grew tall and handsome.

And although Ifan remained the fairy queen's favourite, and she would often come on a moonlit night to watch over him as he lay sleeping, leaving a silver coin under his pillow, never again did she take him away.